Disney · PIXAR

# THE WORLD OF Cars

## "DIRTY JOB"

**RADIATOR SPRINGS** IS LOOKING **GREAT** NOW, **SALLY!**

YEAH, JUST LIKE IN ITS HEYDAY.

EXCEPT FOR OUR POOR LITTLE MURAL...

IT'S IN **REALLY** BAD SHAPE! THE PAINT IS PEELING OFF...

**HEY!** WHAT'S WRONG WITH PEELING PAINT?

UH...NOT **YOU**, MATER. I MEAN...UH...

Radiator Spring
A Happy Place

JUST KIDDING, BUDDY!

HEY, I'VE GOT AN IDEA. LET'S PAINT A **NEW** ONE!

HEY, MAN, I'M ALL FOR IT!

**BAH!** WHAT'S WRONG WITH THE **OLD** ONE?

HUH?

WRITER: ALESSANDRO SISTI    PENCILS: VALENTINO FORLINI    INKS: SONIA MATRONE    COLORS: GIORGIO VALLORANI    LETTERS: MICHAEL STEWART

2

AFTER ALL, WE RENOVATED THE ENTIRE TOWN!

WHY STOP NOW?

IF THAT'S WHAT YOU THINK, THEN GO AHEAD.

YAY!

AWESOME!

YES!

LET'S GET TO IT!

FIRST THINGS FIRST-- A NICE COAT OF WHITE...

...AND NOW IT'S TIME TO PAINT THIS WALL UP RIGHT!

SOON...

UMM... WHAT DO YOU THINK?

I DON'T KNOW... TOO MANY FLAMES!

3

RAMONE, CAN YOU ADD SOME BUMBLEBEES?

I LIKE BUMBLEBEES.

PUT IN SOMETHING THAT WILL LET PEOPLE KNOW THIS IS A PLACE OF PEACE AND ORGANIC LIVING.

BUT *ALSO* A PLACE OF PATRIOTS AND GOOD MORALS!

~GROAN~

OK, IF YOU KNOW IT ALL, WHY DON'T *YOU* HELP ME?

GIVE ME SOME PAINT, HOTSHOT!

*I'LL* HELP YA, HONEY!

THERE CAN NEVER BE TOO MANY FLOWERS!

AND *STARS!*

AND A LOT OF *RED, WHITE, AND BLUE!*

ART WAS BETTER BACK IN THE '20S!

BETTER MAKE THINGS CLEAR FROM THE START.

DONE! ISN'T IT A BEAUTY!

WELL...

⸘UGH⸙ IT'S KIND OF A MESS...

⸘SIGH⸙ IT LOOKS *WORSE* THAN BEFORE!

HEY, MAYBE WHEN IT DRIES IT WILL LOOK DIFFERENT!

WRITER: MICHAEL STEWART   ART: VALENTINO FORLINI   LETTERS: MICHAEL STEWART

LATER, LIGHTNING MCQUEEN HAS A COMMANDING **LEAD** IN THE RACE...

**SPEED!** I **AM** SPEED!

YOU'RE DOING **GREAT**, KID. BUT IT'S TIME FOR A **PIT STOP.**

ALL RIGHT, DOC! BUT THERE ARE ONLY FIVE MORE LAPS LEFT--I THINK I CAN MAKE IT!

YEAH-- THAT'S WHAT YOU **ALWAYS** SAY.

OKAY, MATER, GO OUT THERE AND **SHOW 'EM** WHATCHA GOT.

YOU **GOT IT,** DOC!

NOW YOU FELLERS ARE GONNA **SEE** WHAT A "RUSTY OLD TOW TRUCK" CAN DO!

KA-CHOW!

THIS IS JUST LIKE BEING AT THE **FISHIN' HOLE** BACK HOME!

HUH?

MCQUEEN'S **ACTUALLY** COMING IN FOR A PIT STOP!

YOU **STILL** GLAD TO HAVE HIM ABOARD, HOT ROD?

WELCOME BACK TO THE PIT CREW!

WAY TO GO, MATER!

UH... WELL, I...

AW, SHOOT. YOU'RE GONNA MAKE ME **BLUSH!**

FABULOUS HUDSON HORNET 51

95

THE END!

"A CHASE IN THE DARK!"

EXCELLENT JOB, *DOC.* LISTEN TO MY ENGINE SING!

YOU'RE IN TOP SHAPE!

*VROOOM*

NO CRAZY *HOT-RODDERS* CAN OUTRUN ME NOW.

YOU'RE LOOKING GREAT, *SHERIFF!*

NOT EVEN *MCQUEEN* COULD ESCAPE ME NOW, LIKE HE DID THE *FIRST* TIME WE MET.

IS THAT A JOKE, MAN?

YOU MEAN *OUR* LIGHTNING MCQUEEN?

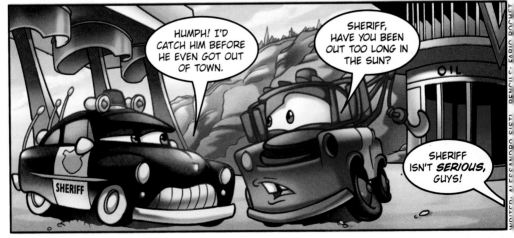

HUMPH! I'D CATCH HIM BEFORE HE EVEN GOT OUT OF TOWN.

SHERIFF, HAVE YOU BEEN OUT TOO LONG IN THE SUN?

SHERIFF ISN'T *SERIOUS,* GUYS!

9

HOW CAN HE BEAT ME? I'M A *RACE CAR!*

YEAH, HE IS A... UH... A "PRE-CISIONAL INSTRUMENT OF SPEED AND AERO-MATICS".

WELL, SO WHAT?

YOU WANT A CHALLENGE? YOU AND I, THE SAME ROAD AS LAST TIME!

C'MON, SHERIFF... I DON'T WANT TO *EMBARRASS* YOU.

OH, WELL, IF YOU'RE NOT UP FOR IT...

FROM THE HIGHWAY BILLBOARD TO THE TELEPHONE POLES.

JUST TRY NOT TO *DESTROY* ANYTHING THIS TIME.

OIL

COOL

OK, IF YOU PUT IT THAT WAY, *I ACCEPT!*

ATTABOY! THERE'S JUST ONE MORE DETAIL...

I'M IN THE LEAD!

I'M ALMOST SORRY TO EMBARRASS THE HOT ROD LIKE THIS, BUT...

...HUH?

VRROOOOOOOOOM

HEY, SHERIFF! DID YOU STOP FOR GAS?

⇒GASP!⇐ YOU WON--AGAIN! I GUESS I CAN'T COMPETE WITH A PISTON CUP CIRCUIT RACER.

HOW DID YOU **DO** IT?

SARGE'S *NIGHT VISION GOGGLES* DEFINITELY HELPED. THANKS, SARGE!

A PLEASURE, PRIVATE!

HA HA! THAT'LL TEACH *ME* TO TALK BIG.

YOU GAVE IT YOUR BEST, SHERIFF--THE OIL'S ON ME.

OR REALLY, ON THE BILL OF MY AGENT, HARV.

THAT'S TALKING LIKE A CHAMP!

LATER . . .

YOU'RE NOT BAD AT ALL, SHERIFF! WHY DON'T YOU TAKE UP RACING?

AND WHAT ABOUT YOU? HAVE YOU EVER THOUGHT OF BECOMING DEPUTY SHERIFF?

OF COURSE, YOU WOULD HAVE TO WORK THE *DAY* SHIFT!

THE END!

**Disney · PIXAR**

**THE WORLD OF Cars**

A QUIET DAY IN *RADIATOR SPRINGS*...

BELLISSIMO!

RADIATOR SPRINGS CURIOS

VREE OM VROOM

**"CLEAN MACHINE!"**

HI THERE, FOLKS! BEAUTIFUL DAY, ISN'T IT?

LIGHTNING! WE HAVEN'T SEEN YOU ALL DAY!

POT POT POT

WOO BOY! THAT DIRT RACING WAS FU-UN! NEXT TIME WE'LL SUIT YOU UP WITH MUD TIRES!

WE NOW BRING YOU THE *FIVE O'CLOCK* NEWS...

UH-OH! I'M LATE! I'VE GOT TO PICK UP SALLY FOR OUR DATE TONIGHT AND...

HERE IT IS

STANLEY USED TO ASK ME OUT ON DATES, BUT *HE* DIDN'T LOOK LIKE SUCH A DUMP!

HUH? MATER, LET ME LOOK IN YOUR MIRROR!

OH, NO!

WRITER: CARLOTTA QUATTROCOLO   PENCILS: VALENTINO FORLINI   INKS: SONIA MATRONE   COLOR: VALENTINO FORLINI   LETTERS: JOHN GREEN

15

HEY!

≈SPLURT≈
THAT'S COLD!

HEY, BUDDY! WE'LL ALL HELP YOU CLEAN UP!

THANKS, RED!

NOW WE NEED A NICE POLISHING!

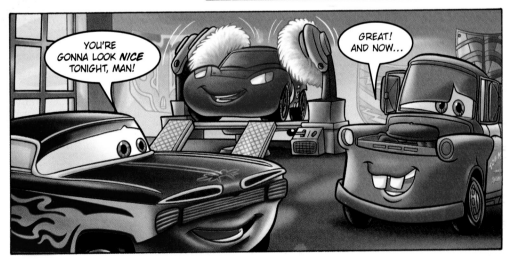

YOU'RE GONNA LOOK NICE TONIGHT, MAN!

GREAT! AND NOW...

"...FOR SOME STYLE!"

PIT STOP!

STANLEY WAS *SO* PERSISTENT! FINALLY I SAID, "ALL RIGHT! *ONE* LITTLE DATE..."

COOL! THANKS, GUYS. I DON'T KNOW WHAT I WOULD HAVE DONE WITHOUT YOU!

WHAT PLANS DO YOU HAVE FOR TONIGHT, ANYWAY?

*PLANS?!* WITH ALL THIS *FUSS* I FORGOT TO MAKE ANY!

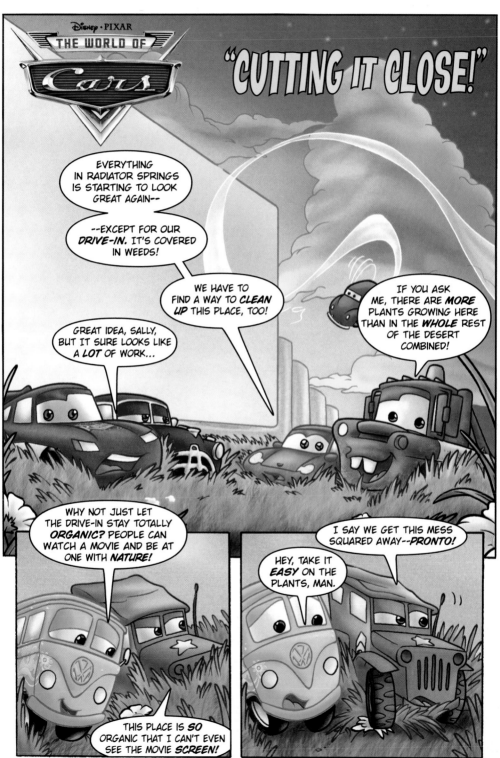

WRITER: MICHAEL STEWART  PENCILS: FABIO POCHET  INKS: RICCARDO SISTI  COLOR: VALENTINO FORLINI  LETTERS: MICHAEL STEWART

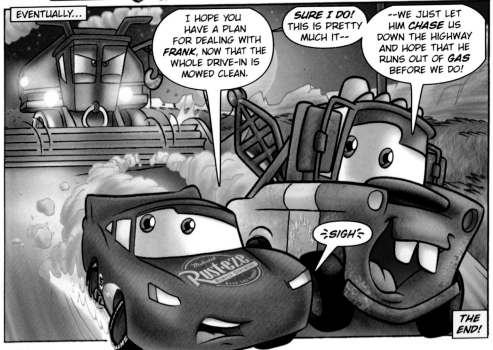

DISNEP · PIXAR
THE WORLD OF
Cars

## "SURPRISE, SURPRISE!"

SINCE SALLY REOPENED THE *WHEEL WELL*, SHE'S ALWAYS IN THERE! WE NEED SOME TIME TO PREPARE EVERYTHING!

WE'VE GOT TO FIND A WAY TO KEEP HER AWAY FOR A WHILE.

YES, BUT *HOW*?

ALL WE NEED TO DO IS FIND SOMETHING SHE'S EVEN *MORE* INTERESTED IN.

AND ACTUALLY, THERE IS SOMETHING... OR RATHER, *SOMEONE!*

UH-OH!

THE NEXT DAY...

*SHERIFF!* WHAT ARE YOU *DOING?*

WRITER: ALESSANDRO SISTI    PENCILS: VALENTINO FORLINI    INKS: RAFFAELLA SECCIA    COLOR: VALENTINO FORLINI    LETTERS: JOHN GREEN

**23**

YOU CAN SEE FOR YOURSELF. I'M *ARRESTING* MCQUEEN!

WHAT FOR? WHAT DID HE DO WRONG?

I DON'T KNOW WHAT'S GOTTEN INTO DOC, BUT HE WENT THROUGH HIS OLD *LAW BOOK*...

"...AND DISCOVERED A BUNCH OF FORGOTTEN LOCAL RULES."

A-HA!

LIKE CODE 6906--IT IS *PROHIBITED* IN RADIATOR SPRINGS TO DRIVE WITHOUT *HEADLIGHTS* AND A *HORN!*

APPARENTLY MY HEADLIGHT STICKERS DON'T COUNT, AND I DON'T HAVE A HORN.

PLUS, CODE 61006-- HIS ENGINE IS *TOO POWERFUL*... AND PLENTY OF OTHER DETAILS.

SO DOC HAS DECIDED TO PUT HIM ON *TRIAL* IMMEDIATELY!

THAT'S CRAZY!

SOON . . .

IT MAY BE CRAZY, BUT IT'S THE *LAW!*

THEN *I'LL* DEFEND HIM.

IMPOSSIBLE! YOU'RE THE PROSECUTOR.

NOT THIS TIME.

I CAN REPLACE YOU, HONEY!

ORDER IN THE COURT! SALLY, DON'T MAKE ME CHARGE YOU WITH CONTEMPT. *LIZZIE*, TAKE YOUR PLACE WITH THE ACCUSED.

LET THE TRIAL BEGIN.

MATER? DO YOU HEAR SOME HOTROD SPEEDERS OUT THERE?

UM, YEAH... WE BETTER GO CATCH 'EM. LET'S GO!

I DON'T BELIEVE THIS. THIS IS CRAZY, *DOC!* HE CAN'T HAVE A FAIR TRIAL UNDER THESE CONDITIONS. IF YOU WANT TO TALK LAW CODES, THEN...

COME ON, QUICK!

THEY'LL BE THERE FOR A WHILE.

MEANWHILE...

DOES THE DEFENDANT PLEAD *GUILTY* OR *INNOCENT?*

WHAT SORT OF A QUESTION IS *THAT*, DOC?

IF ONLY STANLEY WERE HERE, YOU'D ANSWER HIM!

I REMEMBER EYEING STANLEY FROM ACROSS THE COURTROOM. HE WAS A HANDSOME DEVIL...

LIZZIE? STAY *WITH* ME HERE...

ONCE HE ASKED ME TO BE HIS DATE AT A PARTY. HEY, WHEN IS THAT *PARTY* ANYWAY?

PARTY? WHAT PARTY?

LIZZIE MEANT IT WOULD BE A REAL *PARTY* FOR CRIMINALS IF THE LAW WERE NOT RESPECTED!

OF COURSE! EXACTLY!

26

ELSEWHERE...

LET'S HURRY UP!

THE TRIAL WON'T LAST FOREVER!

GRAND OPENING

IN FACT...

DOC! LOOK!

UH... WELL, THE COURT CLOSES AT 4 O'CLOCK. TIME'S UP.

THE CASE IS CLOSED! I PRONOUNCE THE DEFENDANT... *GUILTY!*

WHAAAT?!?

YOU'RE WRONG! I WON'T STAND FOR THIS!

CLANG!

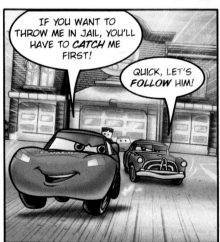

IF YOU WANT TO THROW ME IN JAIL, YOU'LL HAVE TO *CATCH* ME FIRST!

QUICK, LET'S *FOLLOW* HIM!

WAIT FOR ME!

*WHERE ARE THEY GOING?* IT LOOKS LIKE THEY'RE HEADING...

...TOWARD THE **WHEEL WELL**?

FOR SHE'S A JOLLY GOOD FELLOW, FOR SHE'S...

DID YOU FORGET WHAT DAY IT IS TODAY?

OH? I...

IT'S THE **ANNIVERSARY** OF YOUR ARRIVAL IN RADIATOR SPRINGS!

WE WANTED TO THROW YOU A PARTY AT THE SPOT YOU LOVE THE MOST-- WHICH WAS RIGHT HERE.

BUT WE HAD TO KEEP YOU AWAY TO DECORATE IT PROPERLY!

SO YOU SET UP THAT FAKE TRIAL? WHOSE IDEA WAS IT?

HEY, MY ACTING WAS PRETTY GOOD, HUH? MCQUEEN, YOU THINK I COULD GET A PART IN ONE OF THOSE BIG MOVIES?

SINCE I AM THE JUDGE, I CAN CONFESS... WE ARE **ALL** GUILTY!

MATER...

THE END!

28

...THE GREAT RACE CAR **LIGHTNING MCQUEEN** IS NOW STARTING THE LAST LAP AT THE HEAD OF THE RACE.

*Rust-eze*

IT LOOKS LIKE NOTHING CAN STOP HIM FROM WINNING, RIGHT, BOB?

YOU'RE RIGHT, DARRELL--MCQUEEN IS SIMPLY **UNBEATABLE** TODAY, BUT...

... HOLD ON, NOW! WHAT'S GOING ON?

?

I CAN'T BELIEVE MY WINDSCREEN, BOB! MCQUEEN IS GOING IN THE **OPPOSITE** DIRECTION!

VRROOOONNN

IT'S **INCREDIBLE!** EVERYONE IS OVERTAKING HIM. HE'LL END UP **LOSING . . .**

WRITER: ALESSANDRO FERRARI  PENCILS: VALENTINO FERRARI  COLORS: VALENTINO FORLINI  INKS: SONIA MATRONE  COLORS: VALENTINO FORLINI  LETTERS: JOHN GREEN

BUT... WHAT ARE YOU DOING? WHERE ARE YOU *GOING*?

VRROOOOONNN

HOW COULD HE FORGET THAT THE LAST LAP IS RUN IN *REVERSE*?

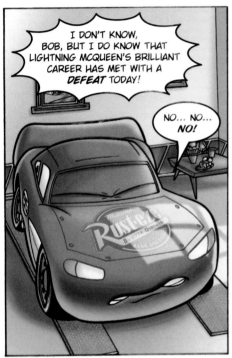

I DON'T KNOW, BOB, BUT I DO KNOW THAT LIGHTNING MCQUEEN'S BRILLIANT CAREER HAS MET WITH A *DEFEAT* TODAY!

NO... NO... *NO!*

WOW...

...IT WAS JUST A DREAM. I REALLY HAVE TO STOP THAT BACKWARDS DRIVING WITH *MATER!*

SPEAKING OF MATER, I'M HAVING BREAKFAST WITH HIM AND SALLY AT FLO'S AND I'M ALREADY LATE!

GOOD THING THAT DRIVING IN THE RIGHT DIRECTION IS THE THING I KNOW HOW TO DO BEST.

NO... IT'S IMPOSSIBLE... THIS IS A *NIGHTMARE!*

SKREEE!

I MUST STILL BE DREAMING-- THANKS TO MATER AND HIS BACKWARDS DRIVING!

WHERE ARE YOU GOING?

I'M GOING BACK TO *SLEEP!* SEE YOU WHEN I WAKE UP... *AGAIN!*

VROOMMM

HEY, DID YOU HEAR THAT, HE THANKED ME! HE REALLY LIKED THE *JOKE,* DIDN'T HE, SALLY?

I'M NOT SO SURE, MATER ... MAYBE THAT WASN'T SO FUNNY AFTER ALL!

THE END!